G. P. PUTNAM'S SONS

A division of Penguin Young Readers Group. Published by The Penguin Group. Penguin Group (USA) Inc., 375 Hudson Street, New York, NY 10014, U.S.A.

Penguin Group (Canada), 90 Eglinton Avenue East, Suite 700, Toronto, Ontario, Canada M4P 2Y3 (a division of Pearson Penguin Canada Inc.).

Penguin Books Ltd, 80 Strand, London WC2R 0RL, England. Penguin Ireland, 25 St. Stephen's Green, Dublin 2, Ireland (a division of Penguin Books Ltd.).

Penguin Group (Australia), 250 Camberwell Road, Camberwell, Victoria 3124, Australia (a division of Pearson Australia Group Pty Ltd).

Penguin Books India Pvt Ltd, 11 Community Centre, Panchsheel Park, New Delhi - 110 017, India.

Penguin Group (NZ), 67 Apollo Drive, Rosedale, North Shore 0745, Auckland, New Zealand (a division of Pearson New Zealand Ltd.).

Penguin Books (South Africa) (Pty) Ltd, 24 Sturdee Avenue, Rosebank, Johannesburg 2196, South Africa.

Penguin Books Ltd, Registered Offices: 80 Strand, London WC2R 0RL, England.

Library of Congress Cataloging-in-Publication Data

Stein, David Ezra.

Monster hug! / David Ezra Stein.   p. cm.

Summary: Two rambunctious young monsters have an action-packed day together.

[1. Monsters–Fiction. 2. Play–Fiction.] I. Title.   PZ7.S8179Mo 2007   [E]–dc22   2007008196

ISBN 978-0-399-24637-1

1 3 5 7 9 10 8 6 4 2

First Impression

To Anne, Matt, and Eva, with love.

SCALY MONSTER

DAVID EZRA STEIN

MONSTER HUG!

G. P. PUTNAM'S SONS

HAIRY MONSTER

MONSTERS MEET

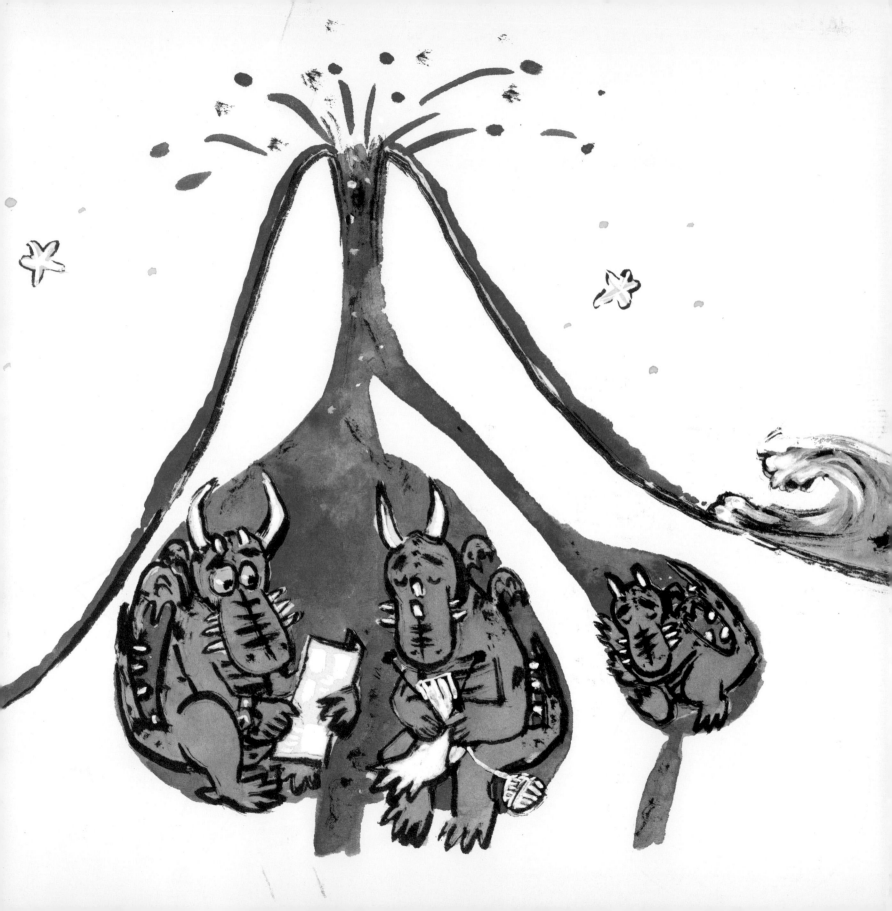